For our friend Kurt, who will never be forgotten

This newly illustrated edition
first published in the United States, Great Britain,
Canada, Australia and New Zealand in 1990 by North-South Books,
an imprint of Nord-Süd Verlag AG, Gossau Zürich, Switzerland.

Text copyright © 1972 by Nord-Süd Verlag AG, Gossau Zürich, Switzerland
Illustrations copyright © 1990 by Nord-Süd Verlag AG, Gossau Zürich, Switzerland
First published in Switzerland under the title *Drei Könige*
English translation copyright © 1990 by Naomi Lewis

Library of Congress Catalog Card Number: 89-43729
ISBN 1-55858-094-8

British Library Cataloguing in Publication Data is available.

1  3  5  7  9  10  8  6  4  2

Printed in Belgium

# THREE KINGS

A Christmas Tale by Kurt Baumann

Illustrated by Ivan Gantschev

TRANSLATED BY NAOMI LEWIS

North-South Books / New York

In a far northern country, long ago, a boy trudged through the frozen countryside. It was almost Christmas time, and in the snow the farmhouses looked like glittering mounds rising out of the earth. In those days there were not so many people about as there are today. There were peasants and there was a king, and there were also people who didn't belong anywhere in particular. They wandered from fair to fair and entertained the village folk with songs and tales and magic tricks. As they were always on the move, they were known as Travellers.

But freezing winter was no time for fairs, and life was hard then for these wanderers. Where could they go? They might beg at farms for a night's lodging, but often farmers were mean and sent them away. It was no laughing matter being a Traveller in winter—and Travellers liked to laugh and be happy and make everyone else laugh too.

One Traveller on his own was a boy called Finju. His long black hair reached his shoulders; he carried a lute, and he played it better than anyone else in the land. Wherever he played, doors were opened; he was given food and a warm welcome. But this year was harder than any he could remember. His fingers were so stiff with cold that he could not pluck the strings. And the farmers kept their doors shut tight.

When evening fell and star after star appeared in the sky, the boy was still trudging through the snow. Little pieces of ice stuck in his hair, and they clinked together like tiny far-off bells. He looked around, both far and wide, but there was not a single house to be seen—just snow, snow, snow, and on the horizon a faint ribbon of sky. Then, some distance away, he saw a figure, a man perhaps, walking across the plain. The boy's heart leapt with hope.

He called out as loudly as he could and hurried towards the stranger. As he came nearer Finju saw a haggard, tall old man in rags. Flung over his shoulders was a tattered coat, hanging in strips down his back—just like a bird's feathers, Finju thought. Then he looked at the old man's face and saw that he was blind.

"Who are you?" said the stranger. He did not open his eyes.

"I am Finju, the lute player," said the boy.

"Finju?" said the old man in surprise. "I know you. You played at the big wedding over there, at Itterby." He put out his hand and tapped the boy on the shoulder. "You are the king of the string players."

"That was a long time ago," said Finju. "But what about you? Who are you?"

"I am Arne," said the old man. "Some call me the beggar king."

Finju remembered: yes, he had heard of a beggar king. It was the title given to an old blind storyteller who was a genius at begging. He did this with such dignity and style that he did not seem an ordinary beggar at all. With his white hair and white beard he really looked more like a king. Only a crown was lacking—and a purple cloak, maybe one, that did not seem like the feathers of a tattered bird.

"But tell me," said the old man, "whatever are you doing here at this unlikely time of year?"

"They are celebrating the Winter Solstice at the royal castle," said Finju. "They call it Yuletide. Perhaps I will have a chance to play there. The farmers have turned me away and my fingers are stiff with cold. But the castle is large; there should be room for strangers, and plenty of light and dancing and merriment."

"Well," said Arne. He sounded cautious. "You don't know the king! Still, at least we are going the same way." He took the boy's arm and they slowly went on together. Walking was difficult. Each step went deep into the snow. They were soon breathing hard. Their footprints were like blurred crooked holes. After a while the old man said, "You may play the lute like a king, but a king shouldn't have a cough like yours, or such icy cold hands—or be wandering about without home or shelter. It isn't right at all."

Finju laughed. "Just wait till we get to the castle. Things will be better then. It will certainly be warm. There'll be feasting too." The thought put him in high spirits, though every step sank deep into the snow. But then a brilliant star appeared in the sky; as it shone the snow froze to a hard crust and walking became very much easier. Now they covered the ground quite quickly.

They walked on without speaking. Once the boy broke the silence. "Arne, please, tell me a story." But the old man said, "I have no stories now. It is twenty years since I told any."

"But why?" begged Finju. "Nothing was worth telling," was all that the old man would say, and the two were silent again.

At last they reached the castle. It was so brightly lit that the snow shone all around. They knocked. The door was opened.

They were shown to a table and they gratefully sat down. It was far from the royal dinner table, but there was wine and roast game, and Arne and Finju hungrily started to eat. But soon they stopped. The desire to eat had left them. And Finju whispered, "Arne, I don't know why, but my fingers still feel frozen." He looked at the courtiers sitting at the royal table, the highest nobles in the land. Yet they were nodding their heads like puppets. All of them sat bent forward, stiffly; it seemed that nobody dared to utter a loud word. You could see a diamond blinking on the king's hand. You could hear the flickering of the candles in the chandelier. Finju's cough could be heard too. Sometimes there was a "Yes, Your Majesty." Then a dead silence again.

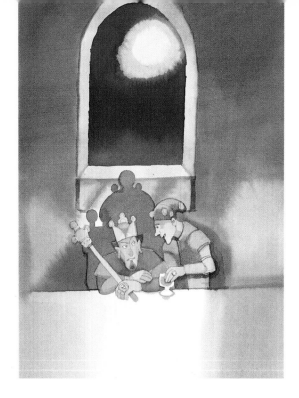

Finju whispered, "The silence outside in the fields was beautiful. But I don't like the silence in this hall. Why is that?" Arne smiled slowly, and said, "Look at the king." Finju did so. The king was reclining dismally in his splendid seat. Then he turned his head to a high official and said in a fretful voice, "They talk about a new star which will appear today. It disturbs me. I don't like new stars; they generally mean change of some sort—a new war, a change in the royal line—disagreeable things of that kind. My subjects should be forbidden to look out for these signs. They stand for rebellion and discontent—I cannot tolerate that. But wait—is this star, perhaps, a fortunate sign for me?"

"Your Majesty," said the official, bowing deeply, "these signs are always difficult to interpret. Tonight's signs are supposed to herald the arrival of a great king. Who else can that be but your royal self? Let us drink to your health and happiness."

All the courtiers rose and sipped at their glasses, which reflected the candlelight. Then the king waved his hand, saying, "The lute player there—tell the lad to play."

There were others in the hall with musical instruments. All were older men, bearded fellows who had come from far away. But all of them looked at Finju. They knew that no one could match his playing.

But Finju coughed and looked downwards. "I can't play here," he whispered to Arne. The king became impatient and stamped his foot. So Finju began to pluck the strings, but the sound was so shrill and false that the courtiers began to laugh and sneer.

Arne rose to his feet. "Your Majesty," he said, "this boy is the finest string player in the land. But his fingers are stiff with cold, and they won't obey him. He crossed the great plain through the snow in the hope of finding warmth, and to bring you music. Be patient a little, and the music will come."

But the king was furious. "What is the use of a player who can't play?" he shouted. "I can't stand whining beggars. Either he plays or I will set the dogs at him." Finju said sadly, "We shall not find any warmth or comfort here." In the babble of scornful laughter he and Arne managed to slip away into the cold outside, without looking back.

There they stood in the snow. Arne said, "We cannot go back across the plain. It is too far. Yet what else can we do? There is no other dwelling of any kind around."

But Finju was gazing at a star which sparkled in the sky and shed a particular brightness on the snow. "Arne," he said. "There is a strange star which seems to point to a path. Let us follow its light."

Arne's eyes were open now, and they reflected the radiance of the star. "I can just see light," he murmured. He was amazed. It was surely a good sign. Finju took his arm, and together they followed the starlit path.

Suddenly they heard a sound, distant at first, then nearer and nearer—the beat of horses' hooves. The starlight shone on a purple cloak; the rider was the king! Behind him rode two strong serving men. "There they are!" thundered the monarch. "Take them prisoner! They have offended me, and they shall suffer for it."

The serving men dismounted from their horses and strode towards the boy and the old man. Arne held out his hands to be chained. "We have done you no harm, Sir King, but by taking us prisoner you may be saving our lives. It is deathly cold out here on the plain, and there is no one to take us in."

The king frowned. "What brought you here anyhow? Where in the devil's name were you going?" "We followed the starlight," Finju said. "Can't you see how brilliant it is? If you wish, Sire, you can come along with us."

The king looked at the star and then at the two wanderers. He sent his servants back to the castle and got down from his horse. "It is strange," he said, "but I would like to come with you. I long to know the meaning of that star."

He took the horse's bridle and together, on foot, the three kings followed the shining path.

Suddenly they came to a building of sorts. It was only a wretched tumbledown hovel, but it stood out in the snow. The icy wind whistled through its cracks and blew the snow inside. The king was puzzled. "I have never seen a house or hut here before," he said. "Shall I knock on the door?"

"No, don't do that," said Finju anxiously. "They might not open the door for you. Let the beggar king knock." So Arne knocked softly on the door. It opened creakingly, and the light of a candle shone on the three outside.

They looked within and wondered. Inside the hut there was nothing—and yet there was something. There was not a stick of furniture, only a rough cradle, over which a poorly dressed woman was bending. By the door stood a man. "Welcome!" he said.

Then, in the cradle, they perceived the child. It was wrapped in rags; it looked very cold. Arne said a strange thing—though they did not realize how strange it was until afterwards. "I can see you!" he said. "You are brighter than the star we followed!" He took the sheepskin tied around his waist and gently laid it over the child.

The best that Finju had to give was his music. He took his lute, and now his fingers played as never before. And when he had finished, the king took the golden chain from his own neck and placed it at the foot of the cradle. "I never knew," he said, "that there were such poor people in my country. I must take more care of them."

Then Arne said to Finju, "Now do you know why we crossed the great plain?" Finju replied, "You need not tell me *this* story, Arne. But it will be your best through all the years to come."